This Little Tiger book belongs to:

_____

_____

_____

_____

For Mum and Dad, with love
~J.S.

For Alice, who helped
with the painting, Katy, and Mark
~T.W.

LITTLE TIGER PRESS
An imprint of Magi Publications
1 The Coda Centre, 189 Munster Road,
London SW6 6AW, UK
www.littletigerpress.com

First published in Great Britain 1999
by Little Tiger Press, London
This edition published 2008

Printed in China

2 4 6 8 10 9 7 5 3 1

Little Tiger's big surprise!

by Julie Sykes

Pictures by Tim Warnes

LITTLE TIGER PRESS

Little Tiger was very happy being an only tiger, so when Mommy Tiger said, "There's going to be a new baby, you'll have a little brother or a little sister," Little Tiger answered,

"But I don't want a new baby.
I like things the way they are."

Little Tiger thought that if he didn't mention the
new baby, Mommy Tiger would change her mind.
So he was very upset when one day she said,
"The new baby will be here soon."

Little Tiger stamped his paw.
"I don't *want* a new baby," he shouted,
and off he ran into the jungle
to find his friends.

Little Tiger went to call on Little Elephant, but to his dismay, Little Elephant didn't want to play.

"I'm teaching my baby brother how to squirt water," he trumpeted.

The baby elephant wasn't very good at it.
Instead of sending a jet of water into the river,
he kept dribbling it all over himself.

"*Yucky!*" thought Little Tiger. "I don't want
a little brother if he dribbles."

Little Tiger scampered on until he spotted Little Monkey. "Come and play with me," he called.

But Little Monkey didn't have time to play. "I'm teaching my baby brother how to eat," he explained.

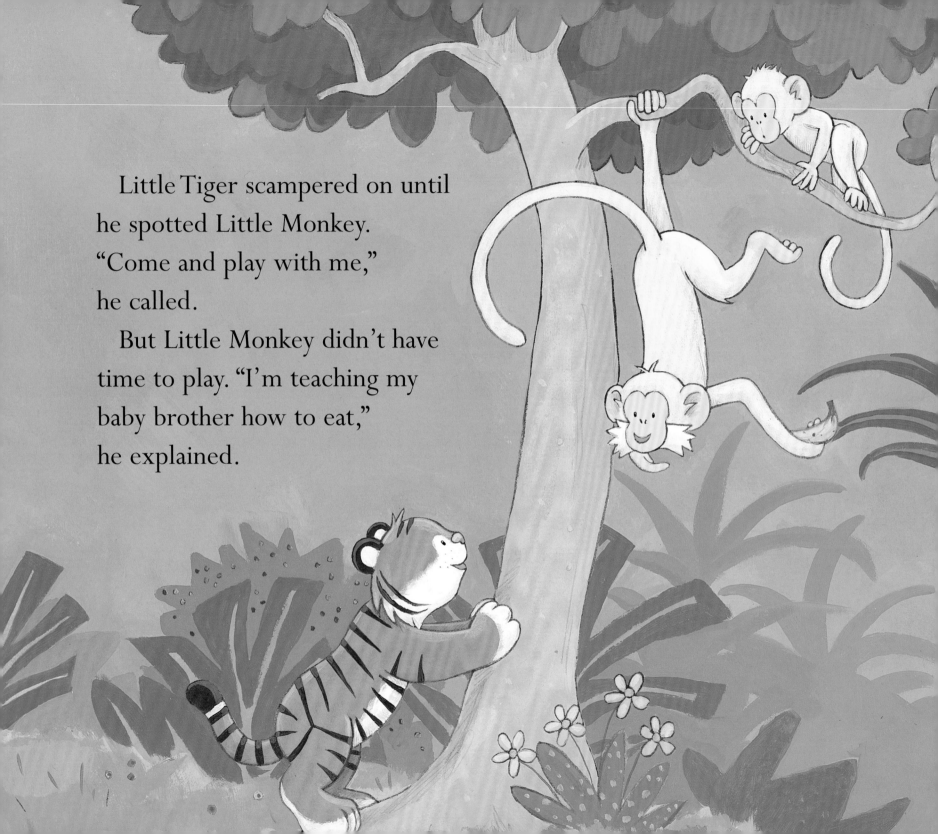

Little Tiger watched, and soon both Little Monkey and the baby were covered in sticky banana.

"*Ugh, ugh!*" said Little Tiger to himself. "I don't want a little brother if he eats like that."

Little Tiger hurried on and soon he came across Little Bear. She was holding something over her shoulder.

"I'm burping our new baby," she told him.

Little Tiger waited, and suddenly the baby
was sick all down Little Bear's back. Little
Tiger's nose twitched in disgust.

"Phooey!" he growled. "I don't want a little
brother if he does that."

Just then, Little Tiger spotted Little Parrot,
but Little Parrot was far too busy to play
with her friend.

"We've got some new babies," she said.
"They've just hatched, and I'm looking after
them while Mommy Parrot rests."

Little Tiger peered into the nest. The babies were very ugly.
Their beaks were too large and their feathers all crumpled.
"How nice," he said politely, but he didn't stop to admire
them for long. "I don't want a little brother if he looks like
they do," he said as he scurried on through the jungle.

Suddenly Little Tiger heard a loud snore.
Who could it be?

It was Little Rhino, fast asleep in the shade.
"Wake up, Little Rhino, it's the middle of the day,"
he shouted. Sleepily Little Rhino opened her eyes.
"We've got a new baby," she said, yawning. "She cries
a lot and keeps me awake at night."

Little Tiger didn't like the sound of that. He didn't
want to fall asleep in the lovely sunshine! "If that's what
babies do, then I don't want one," he thought sadly.

Little Tiger wasn't very happy. Babies were even worse than he'd imagined! They took up everyone's time and they did horrible things. "I'd much rather be an only tiger," he thought as he trotted home.

On the way, he met Daddy Tiger,
pacing the jungle floor.
"Why the sad face?" asked Daddy Tiger.
"What's wrong?"

"Babies are horrible," said Little Tiger. "I don't want one."
Sadly, he told Daddy Tiger about all the things he'd seen
other babies do.

When he'd finished, Daddy Tiger said, "New babies do
have some messy habits, but they soon grow out of
them. You were a baby once, but you're not so bad now."

It made Little Tiger laugh to think that he'd been a baby tiger, too.

"It will be good fun having a new baby," said Daddy Tiger. "You'll see."

Little Tiger followed Daddy Tiger through the jungle. Back at the den, Mommy Tiger was very excited.

"The new baby has arrived," she whispered.

Little Tiger crept inside the den and there, curled up on a bed of leaves, he found . . .

. . . the baby tiger!

Little Tiger stared. His baby brother wasn't at all what he'd expected. The new baby was just a tiny copy of himself! Suddenly, Little Tiger felt very pleased and proud.

But Mommy and Daddy Tiger had another surprise for Little Tiger . . .

"How do you like your baby sister?" asked Daddy Tiger.

"A *sister!*" exclaimed Little Tiger.

He looked at the baby again. Would she be fun? He'd have to wait and see.

"I do like my little sister," said Little Tiger. And then he added, "But can I have a baby brother next time?"

fantastic reads from Little Tiger Press

BEWARE of the BEARS!
Alan MacDonald
Gwyneth Williamson

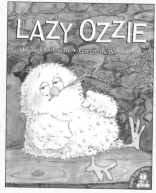

LAZY OZZIE
Michael Coleman • Gwyneth Williamson

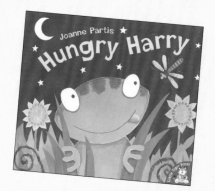

Joanne Partis
Hungry Harry

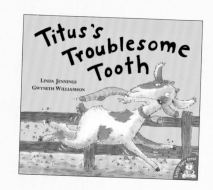

Titus's Troublesome Tooth
LINDA JENNINGS
GWYNETH WILLIAMSON

Little Tiger's big surprise!
Julie Sykes • Tim Warnes

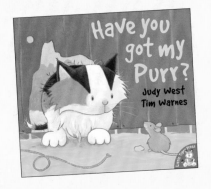

Have you got my Purr?
Judy West
Tim Warnes

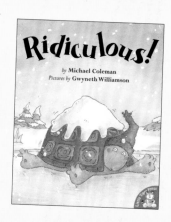

Ridiculous!
by Michael Coleman
Pictures by Gwyneth Williamson

Martin Hall and Catherine Walters
Charlie and Tess

For information regarding any of the above titles
or for our catalogue, please contact us:
Little Tiger Press, 1 The Coda Centre,
189 Munster Road, London SW6 6AW, UK
Tel: +44 (0)20 7385 6333 Fax: +44 (0)20 7385 7333
E-mail: info@littletiger.co.uk
www.littletigerpress.com

IT COULD HAVE BEEN WORSE
A.H. Benjamin • Tim Warnes

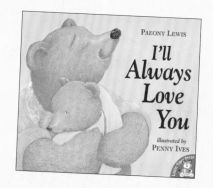

PAEONY LEWIS
I'll Always Love You
illustrated by
PENNY IVES